BARTHOLOMEW

and the

BUG

by Neal Layton

Bartholomew lived in a cave in a forest at the top of a mountain.

He spent his days sniffing flowers, snoozing in leafy glades, snacking on berries and generally taking it nice and easy.

But sometimes in the evenings he would climb up to the top of the cliff and watch the twinkling lights down in the valley below. He wondered what they were, and what went on there. Perhaps he would go there tomorrow, or sometime next week...

One day whilst he was reclining
in his favourite spot a
strange little bug flew up
and hit him on the nOse.

It spoke very quickly in a squeaky voice and kept gasping for breath, but eventually Bartholomew managed to work out what it was saying.

Bartholomew led the bug over to the edge of the cliff to show him where the twinkling lights were down in the valley,

but every couple of paces
the little bug got
caught up by the **wind** and would end up **flying**
in a completely different direction.

AGHHHHHH!
BUZZ!

PLEEEZE
CAN YOU
HELP ME
MR BEAR?

PLEEEZE??

BUZZZ.

AGHHHH!

It seemed obvious the little creature couldn't do this alone

and being a kindly bear, with nothing

much in particular planned

for the day, **Bartholomew**

agreed to

help him in

his
quest.

They
didn't have

a second
to lose.

Cradling the small insect in his big paws Bartholomew clambered his way to the bottom of the cliff.

A frog directed them through the stinking swamps.

And over the w a t e r f a l l s.

Until eventually they arrived at a **huge** concrete road.

Bartholomew was devastated.

He couldn't read that well but he knew that 117 was a very **big** number, and so 117 miles must be a **very** long way, and that a very long way was sure to take **much** more than a day to walk. They'd never make it in time.

He sat down by the edge of the road with the bug in the palm of his paw. He didn't know how he would tell him the bad news.

Just then a huge truck pulled up and a hairy-faced man got out, stood beside the road and began to whistle.

Bartholomew and the bug very quietly tiptoed
out from the undergrowth, climbed on to the back
of the truck and hid behind some big boxes.

Neither Bartholomew nor the bug had ever travelled **SO** fast in their lives.

They were there in record-breaking time.
The truck screeched to a halt and Bartholomew
and the bug hopped down to take their first
glimpse of the bright lights of the big city.

But it wasn't what they were expecting at all.
There weren't any bright lights, only tall
grey buildings.

WELCOME TO THE BIG CITY

RESTAURANT FOOD SNACKS

They must have got it wrong somehow.
There weren't any lights anywhere.

The bug tried to hide his disappointment.

But as they wandered through the streets and alleys they began to notice a few twinkling lights appearing: first one, then two, then more and more.

Until the whole place was awash with luminescent glow.
And with the lights came the buzz of thousands of insects of every shape and size, all here for the same reason: TO PARTY!

They sang.

They danced till Bartholomew thought his legs would drop off

and some of the bug's did!

And just as Bartholomew thought he could dance
no more and the first whispers of dawn began to
peep their way over the horizon, he noticed the bug
staring into the eyes of a rather pretty lady-bug, and
he thought it was probably time for him to go home.

Bartholomew bade farewell to his
insect friends and thanked
them for such a wonderful day.
Until with a FRIZZLE-FRAZZLE
sound they were gone altogether.

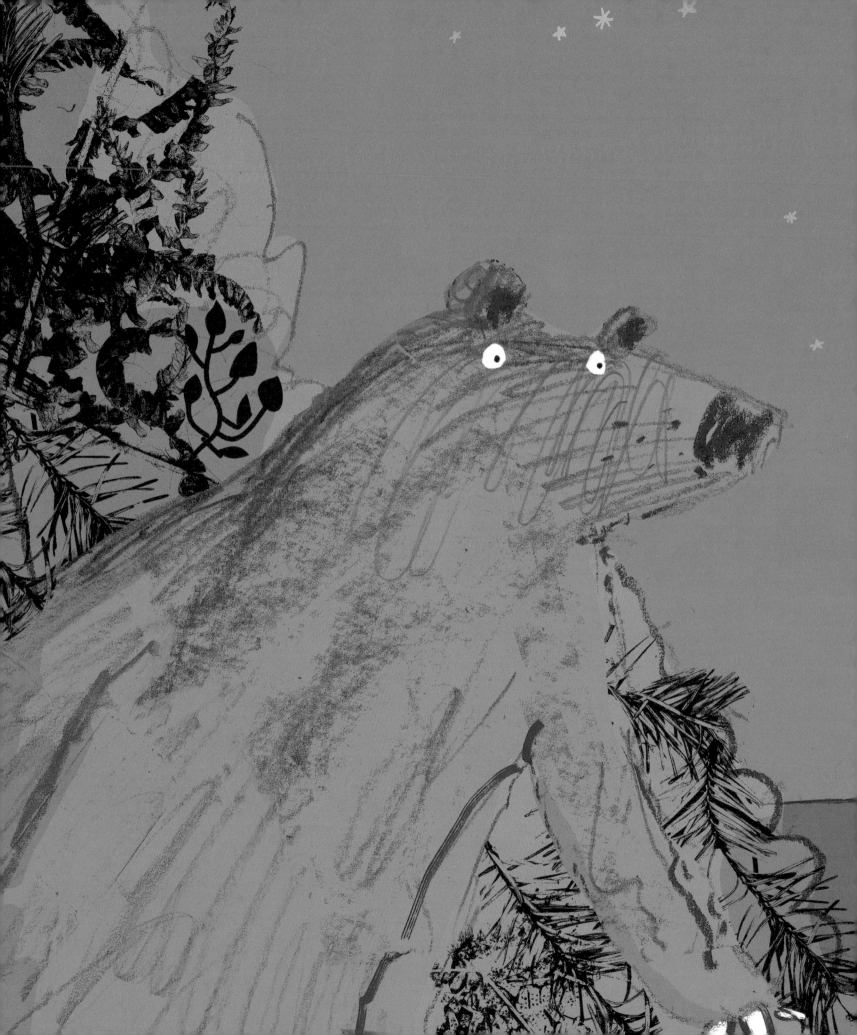

Bartholomew never went back to the bright lights of the big city.

But at the end of each day, when he sits and watches them from his mountain top, he always thinks of his little bug friend and the fantastic day they spent there together.

BEAR FACTS GRIZZLY BEARS

ARE FOUND IN WESTERN NORTH AMERICA, MAINLY IN MOUNTAINOUS REGIONS. THEY SPEND MOST OF THEIR LIVES AS SOLITARY NOMADS MOSEYING AROUND THEIR RANGE, TRAVELLING KNOWN TRAILS, SEEKING KNOWN REPOSITORIES OF FOOD AND FINDING SECLUDED DAYBEDS FOR SNOOZING. GRIZZLY BEARS CAN LIVE FOR UP TO 25 YEARS.

BUG FACTS CRANE-FLIES

ARE VERY COMMON. THEY SPEND MOST OF THEIR LIVES AS LARVAE BENEATH THE GROUND, EVENTUALLY EMERGING AS ADULTS IN LATE SUMMER AND EARLY FALL. THEY DO NOT FEED NOR DO THEY BITE OR STING. THEIR UNGAINLY FLIGHTS ARE THOUGHT TO ACT AS BOTH A SOCIAL ACTIVITY AND AN AWKWARD KIND OF COURTSHIP DISPLAY. THEY ARE ATTRACTED TO LIGHTS AND MAY GET INTO THE HOUSE BY MISTAKE WHERE THEY GENERALLY DIE. CRANE-FLY ADULTS ONLY LIVE FOR ONE OR TWO DAYS AT MOST. IN ENGLAND THEY CARRY THE COMMON NAME OF DADDY-LONG-LEGS.

BOOK FACTS

NEAL GOT THE IDEA FOR THIS BOOK WHILST CAMPING IN THE SIERRA NEVADA MOUNTAINS. HE DIDN'T SEE ANY BEARS BUT SAW PLENTY OF BUGS. THIS BOOK IS DEDICATED TO ALL THE LITTLE CREATURES OF THE WORLD.

BARTHOLOMEW AND THE BUG BY NEAL LAYTON

British Library Cataloguing in Publication Data. A catalogue record of this book is available from the British Library.

ISBN 978 0 340 98933 3